SCHOLASTIC

icky sticky readers

Brilliant Bats

Laaren Brown

SCHOLASTIC INC.

New York   Toronto   London   Auckland
Sydney   Mexico City   New Delhi   Hong Kong

Dear family of new readers,

Welcome to Icky Sticky Readers, part of the Scholastic Reader program. At Scholastic, we have taken over ninety years' worth of experience with teachers, parents, and children and put it into a program that is designed to match your child's interest and skills. Scholastic Readers are designed to support your child's efforts to learn how to read at every age and every stage.

LEVEL 1 READER
- Beginning Reader
- Preschool–Grade 1
- Sight words
- Words to sound out
- Simple sentences

LEVEL 2 READER
- Developing Reader
- Grades 1–2
- New vocabulary
- Longer sentences

LEVEL 3 READER
- Growing Reader
- Grades 1–3
- Reading for inspiration and information

For ideas about sharing books with your new reader, please visit www.scholastic.com.

ICKY STICKY STICKERS

Every time you see this bat symbol, look for a sticker to fill the space!

Contents

Copyright © 2016 by Scholastic Inc.

All rights reserved. Published by Scholastic Inc., *Publishers since 1920.* SCHOLASTIC and associated logos are trademarks and/or registered trademarks of Scholastic Inc.

No part of this publication may be reproduced, stored in a retrieval system, or transmitted in any form or by any means, electronic, mechanical, photocopying, recording, or otherwise, without written permission of the publisher. For information regarding permission, write to Scholastic Inc., Attention: Permissions Department, 557 Broadway, New York, NY 10012.

ISBN 978-0-545-93550-0

12 11 10 9 8 7 6 5 4 3 2 1   16 17 18 19 20 21/0

Printed in the U.S.A.   40
First edition, July 2016

Scholastic is constantly working to lessen the environmental impact of our manufacturing processes. To view our industry-leading paper procurement policy, visit www.scholastic.com/paperpolicy.

Brilliant bats

You think all bats are scary bloodsuckers?
Well, some of them are! But many, many more
eat nothing but bugs or fruit. Here come
some BRILLIANT bats. Here's a huge fruit bat.
There's a teeny-weeny bumblebee bat.
Here's an orange bat, and a bat
that hovers.

READY? SET?
LET'S FLY!

fruit bat's wingspan: **5 feet**

bumblebee bat's wingspan: **5 inches**

Like us, bats are mammals. They provide milk for their babies. Unlike us, bats can FLY! Their hands are their wings. They have very long finger bones. A thin layer of skin, called a membrane, stretches between the bones.

A bat's hand has four long fingers and a short thumb.

fruit bat

When they fly, bats don't flap like birds do. They SCOOP their wings forward. Some bats scoop up tasty bugs as they fly!

IS IT A BIRD?

IS IT A PLANE?

NO! I'M THE ONLY FLYING MAMMAL!

7

Batty roosts

Bats are the original party animals. It's easy for them—they're NOCTURNAL. That means that they sleep all day. Then, when the sun sets, they fly off for a night out. When the sun rises, many bats roost (settle down for a snooze). They roost upside down in caves, trees, attics, or even spiderwebs!

ICKY STICKY STICKERS

Some bats like to roost in buildings.

TREE ROOSTS

fruit bats

A bat might cling to a leaf . . .

. . . chew a leaf to make a tent . . .

. . . or roost on a tree trunk.

A bamboo bat roosts inside a bamboo stalk.

To the bat cave! Bats and caves go together like gardens and guano. What's guano? BAT POOP! Caves are nice and dark, with plenty of space. But is sleeping upside down tricky? Not for a bat! When the bat sleeps, its claws shut tightly. This lets the bat hold on until it's time to wake up. Then it DROPS into flight.

Guano can be spread on soil to help plants grow.

60 feet: depth of guano in Bracken Cave, TX

clingy claws

greater
horseshoe bat

ICKY STICKY STICKERS

In winter, this bat sleeps in a cave to save energy.

On a warm summer day, at Bracken Cave
in Texas, all is quiet . . . until dusk falls.
Then—WHOOOOOSH! The sky fills with **MEXICAN
FREE-TAILED BATS**—about 20 million of them!

This is the world's LARGEST bat colony. The bats fly out in search of mosquitoes and moths. Those bugs better LOOK OUT! These are some of the fastest bats in the world. They can fly 60 miles per hour. Together, they can eat up to 250 tons of bugs in a single night!

Say it

colony
(say KAH-luh-nee)
A large group of animals that live together.

New word

TRAFFIC JAM!

13

Echo-o-o-o

Bats live in darkness. Why don't they bump into things? They don't need light to see where they're going. They use sound. Echolocation lets bats HEAR what's around them. This **VESPER BAT** is squeaking.

It listens to the squeaks ECHO off, or bounce back from, objects all around. The echoes help the bat figure out where everything is—trees, other bats, and that tasty moth. Bats have wrinkles and flaps on their heads to help them make or hear squeaks.

BATTY BITS FOR ECHOLOCATION

small flap at the front of each large ear

pointed flap of skin on the nose

nose flap shaped like a horseshoe

ICKY STICKY STICKERS

A gray long-eared bat has big ears. How big? Big enough to tuck under its wings at nap time!

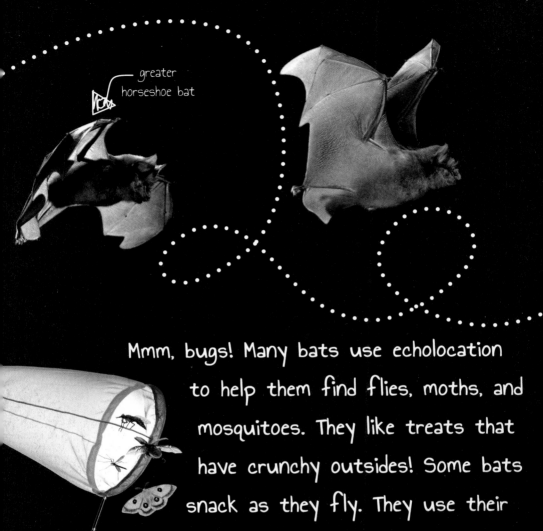

greater horseshoe bat

Mmm, bugs! Many bats use echolocation to help them find flies, moths, and mosquitoes. They like treats that have crunchy outsides! Some bats snack as they fly. They use their wing and tail membranes as nets. They catch and scoop bugs into their mouths. Others carry their prey home and eat there. The woolly bat folds up its tail membrane like a bib to catch bits of food.

This bulldog bat has a
face like a bulldog's!

woolly bat

Here's a bat that doesn't bother with insects. It's got bigger FISH to fry! The **GREATER BULLDOG BAT** is a fantastic fisher. It flies in circles high up in the air. It uses echolocation to find ripples in water below. AHA! A FISH!

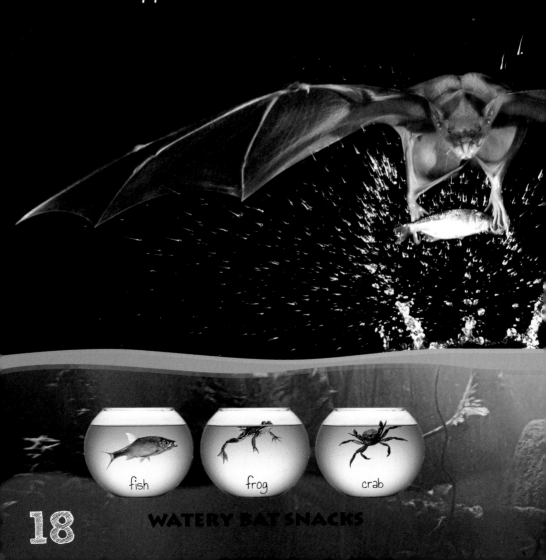

fish   frog   crab

WATERY BAT SNACKS

The bat swoops low, skimming the surface. Then it snatches the fish out of the water, using its big feet. CHOW TIME!

Say it

insect
(say *IN-sekt*)
A small animal with six legs, wings, and a tough outer skeleton.

New word

ICKY STICKY STICKERS

The frog-eating bat eats insects, lizards, and—you guessed it—frogs!

19

Batty dinners

Love fruit flavors? So do . . . **FRUIT BATS!**
Nicknamed "flying foxes," these big boys and girls
are not good at echolocation. They don't have the
huge ears and wrinkles that other bats use to
catch bugs. Instead, they use their large EYES
and NOSES to find yummy bananas or figs.
Most fruit bats have LOOOONNNNG tongues
to reach into flowers and lap up sweet nectar.

straw-colored
fruit bat

Some bats can HOVER like hummingbirds. They hover near flowers to sip the nectar. Then they eat the powdery pollen that sticks to their fur.

FRUIT BAT MENU

fruit

flower nectar

leaves

flower buds

flower pollen

21

For this bat, there is only one thing on the menu. BLOOD. When night falls, the **VAMPIRE BAT** sails into the darkness. It listens for the sounds of a sleeping animal—a pig, horse, or cow. Then—OPEN WIDE. It's tooth time!

WELCOME TO MY FANG CLUB!

The bat stabs into the animal
with its sharp fangs. Blood
flows, and the bat laps it up.
Sometimes the bat drinks
for 30 minutes. JUICY!

Vampire bats are
named after the
famous monsters,
like the one in the
story *Dracula.*

Face it: The vampire bat is CREEPY. Unlike most other bats, it can move quickly on all fours. The bat CREEPS and CRAWLS over its victim. A heat sensor in its nose helps it find warm blood just below the skin. Some blood donors never know that they've been bitten. Others DIE . . .

The bat pees after feeding. Then it's light enough to fly!

SO LONG, SUCKERS!

ICKY STICKY STICKERS

The white-winged vampire bat can shoot stinky liquid from its mouth.

A bat's life

They look like aliens, but bats are mammals. This means that a baby bat is born LIVE. It does not hatch from an egg. It also means that it drinks its mother's milk (even vampire bats do). Some babies cling to mom's tummy as she flies.

GROWING UP

1

Newborn bats are often bald.

2

Hold on tight, baby!

size: **1 inch**

baby bat

Some stay at home, huddling with other babies. Right from birth, their legs and claws are strong enough for roosting upside down. After about one month of babyhood, most bats are ready for life on the wing.

3

Baby bats hang out together.

4

Flying high next to mom!

ICKY STICKY STICKERS

These baby fruit bats needed a little TLC— tender loving care. Their home was destroyed by floods. They'll be released soon.

TOP 10 brilliant bats

Bats are BRILLIANT! They hang upside down, they love nighttime, and they can fly. And some of them live on all-blood diets! Which bat is your favorite?

fruit bat

4

greater bulldog bat

5

geoffroy's tailless bat

6

gray long-eared bat

7

bumblebee bat

8

ghost bat

9

hairless bulldog bat

10

painted bat

ICKY STICKY STICKERS

This fruit bat is totally white in color.

Glossary

bloodsucker
An animal that drinks blood.

colony
A large group of animals that live together.

echo
To bounce back a sound from an object.

echolocation
A way that an animal can find food and other objects in the dark. The animal makes sounds that bounce off the objects and echo back to the animal.

fang
An animal's long, pointed tooth.

guano
Bat poop.

hover
To stay in one place in the air.

huddle
To come together in a close group.

insect
A small animal with six legs, wings, and a tough outer skeleton.

lap
To drink liquid quickly with the tongue.

mammal
An animal that breathes air and usually gives birth to live babies. Mother mammals make milk to feed their babies. Humans and bats are mammals.

membrane
A thin sheet or layer of skin.

nectar
A sweet liquid made by plants. Bats, bees, and butterflies drink nectar.

nocturnal
Awake at night.

pollen
The tiny yellow grains made by flowers.

prey
An animal that is hunted and eaten by another animal.

roost
To settle somewhere to rest or sleep.

sensor
A body part on an animal that can help it find or notice something. A vampire bat's heat sensor helps it find warm blood.

skim
To pass quickly and lightly across something.

wingspan
The distance from the end of one wing to the end of the other wing.

WHY AM I ALONE?

I MUST HAVE BAT BREATH!

Index

Image credits

Photographs © : cover background: Browinstock/Alamy Images; cover bat: Olaf Wagner/ullstein bild/Getty Images; cover cartoon: Cory Thoman/iStockphoto; back cover cartoon: Cory Thoman/iStockphoto; back cover center right: Faultier/iStockphoto; back cover center left: Corina daniela Obertas/Dreamstime; back cover top left: adrianciurea/a/iStockphoto; 1 main and sticker: Cucu Remus/iStockphoto; 1 top left cartoon hat and throughout: Sarawut Padungkwan/123RF; 1 top right cartoon: Igor Zakowski/123RF; 2–3 top background: Steve Guest/Dreamstime; 2–3 bottom background: Andreluc88/Dreamstime; 2 bat silo and throughout and stickers: DeCe_X/iStockphoto; 2 bottom left bat and sticker: Isselee/Dreamstime; 2 bottom left stone: Pop Nukoonrat/Dreamstime; 3 top and sticker: Allard1/Dreamstime; 3 center right and sticker: ivkuzmin/iStockphoto; 3 bottom left: Zhu Zihong/123RF; 3 bat silos and throughout and stickers: Mtkang/Dreamstime; 4–5 background: Dave Bredeson/Dreamstime; 4 bottom and sticker: Faultier/iStockphoto; 4 center top and sticker: rpbirdman/iStockphoto; 4 center bottom and sticker: ivkuzmin/iStockphoto; 5 top left: ivkuzmin/iStockphoto; 5 center top: Stephen Dalton/Science Source; 5 center bottom and sticker: Craig Dingle/iStockphoto; 5 bottom left: Nicolas Reusens/Getty Images; 5 bottom right: Dr. Merlin D. Tuttle/Science Source; 6–7 background: Sinakamo/Dreamstime; 6–7 bat and stickers: Craig Dingle/iStockphoto; 6 left center and sticker: Rose Waddell/Dreamstime; 6 photo corners and throughout: hanibaram/iStockphoto; 7 top right moon and throughout: Marko/Dreamstime; 7 bottom left cartoon: lineartestpilot/123RF; 7 bottom right cartoon bat and throughout: Sarawut Padungkwan/123RF; 8–9 background: Karaket74/Dreamstime; 8 center left: Cucu Remus/iStockphoto; 8 wooden beam: Rawpixelimages/Dreamstime; 8 far left bat: Cucu Remus/iStockphoto; 8 all other bats: adrianciurea/a/iStockphoto; 8 center bat and sticker: adrianciurea/a/iStockphoto; 8 right bat and sticker: adrianciurea/a/iStockphoto; 8 far right bat: adrianciurea/a/iStockphoto; 9 top: Craig Dingle/iStockphoto; 9 bamboo: Paul Cowan/Dreamstime; 9 bottom right bat: Dr. Merlin D. Tuttle/Science Source; 9 center left: Christian Ziegler/Getty Images; 9 center right: Vilainecrevette/Dreamstime; 9 bottom left: Brian Lasenby/123RF; 10 top: 11 background: Cucu Remus/iStockphoto; 10–11 bottom right cartoon: Yael Weiss/123RF; 11 foreground bat and sticker: adrianciurea/a/iStockphoto; 11 magnifying glass: Billyfoto/Dreamstime; 11 top claws: Dr. Merlin D. Tuttle/Science Source; 12 background: Nature Picture Library/Alamy Images; 12 foreground bat: Joel Sartore/Getty Images; 13 bottom cartoon: RitToon/iStockphoto; 13 background: Nature Picture Library/Alamy Images; 14–15 background: Constantin Opris/Dreamstime; 14 bat: Paul Van Hoof/Buiten-beeld/Getty Images; 14 moth: Antagain/iStockphoto; 15 frames and stickers: Iakov Filimonov/Dreamstime; 15 left bat and sticker: ecomike/iStockphoto; 15 center bat and sticker: Atelopus/iStockphoto; 15 right bat and sticker: ivkuzmin/iStockphoto; 16–17 grass: George Tsartsianidis/Dreamstime; 16 top: Stephen Dalton/Getty Images; 16 net: Antagain/iStockphoto; 16 fly: DrPAS/iStockphoto; 16 mosquito: alexnika/iStockphoto; 16 beetle: defun/iStockphoto; 16 moth: Gusa Mihai Cristian/Dreamstime; 16 bottom left cartoon: Igor Zakowski/123RF; 17 top right: Stephen Dalton/Getty Images; 17 bottom right: Dr. Merlin D. Tuttle/Science Source; 17 top left: Stephen Dalton/Getty Images; 18–19 bottom background: Melissa King/Dreamstime; 18 center: Christian Ziegler/Getty Images; 18 fish bowls: Valergilda/iStockphoto; 18 bottom fish: GlobalP/iStockphoto; 18 bottom frog: GlobalP/iStockphoto; 18 bottom crab: eye-blink/iStockphoto; 19 center right cartoon rod: sunstock/iStockphoto; 19 center right cartoon fish: Popmarleo/iStockphoto; 19 bottom left fish: Isselee/Dreamstime; 19 bottom center fish: Isselee/Dreamstime; 19 center left: Christian Ziegler/Getty Images; 20–21 background: Liljam/Dreamstime; 20 bottom and sticker: Ivkuzmin/Dreamstime; 21 top left: Nicolas Reusens/Getty Images; 21 top right leaves: fluxfoto/iStockphoto; 21 bottom right leaves: fluxfoto/iStockphoto; 21 center left leaves: genphoto_art/iStockphoto; 21 bottom right cactus: TonyMarinella/iStockphoto; 21 bottom left: Tanantornanutra/iStockphoto; 21 center nectar: ecosflora/Alamy Images; 21 center left figs: Anna Kucherova/iStockphoto; 21 center left banana: KRU5/iStockphoto; 21 center left papaya: LuVo/iStockphoto; 21 center left leaves: rodno/iStockphoto; 21 bottom menu background: Naddya/iStockphoto; 21 center cartoon silverware: Igor Zakowski/Dreamstime; 21 bottom right pollen: Lokibaho/iStockphoto; 22 bottom: Michael & Patricia Fogden/Getty Images; 22–23 blood spots: yukipon/Shutterstock, Inc.; 23 background: Igorzh/Dreamstime; 23 dracula: Albert Ziganshin/Shutterstock, Inc.; 23 center bat silo and stickers: Dkvektor/Dreamstime; 23 top right blood: freelancebloke/iStockphoto; 24–25 bottom: Oxford Scientific/Getty Images; 25 bat: Dr. Merlin D. Tuttle/Science Source; 25 wood sign: janniwet/iStockphoto; 25 people silos: Pillon/iStockphoto; 26–27 bottom background: Kirsty Pargeter/Dreamstime; 26 bottom left: Corina daniela Obertas/Dreamstime; 26 center left: PlazacCameraman/iStockphoto; 26 center right: ivkuzmin/Dreamstime; 27 center left: Dr. Merlin D. Tuttle/Science Source; 27 center right: Dr. Merlin D. Tuttle/Science Source; 27 top right bat: Faultier/iStockphoto/Thinkstock; 28–29 top background: Satit Srihin/Dreamstime; 28 top left bat: Tony Camacho/Science Source; 28–29 medals: _human/iStockphoto; 28 top right bat: Joel Sartore/Getty Images; 29 top center bat: roberthardimg/Alamy Images; 29 top left bat: Tharvron Posri/Dreamstime; 29 hairless bulldog bat and sticker: Dr. Merlin D. Tuttle/Science Source; 29 ghost bat: B. G. Thomson/Science Source; 29 painted bat and sticker: PITOON KITRATANASAK/Shutterstock, Inc.; 29 gray long-eared bat and sticker: Isselee/Dreamstime; 29 greater bulldog bat: Christian Ziegler/Getty Images; 29 nectar-feeding bat: Nicolas Reusens/Getty Images; 29 bumblebee bat: Dr. Merlin D. Tuttle/Science Source; 30–31: Moreno Novello/Dreamstime; 32 background: Pavlo Vakhrushev/Dreamstime; 32 bottom left: Stevenrussellsmithphotos/Dreamstime; 32 bottom right and sticker: ivkuzmin/Dreamstime; vampire bat sticker: Oxford Scientific/Getty Images; bat sleeping in a cave sticker: David Parsons/Dreamstime; white-winged vampire bat sticker: Rexford Lord/Science Source; baby fruit bats sticker: Newspix/Getty Images; white fruit bat sticker: Абаджева Марина/123RF; frog-eating bat sticker: Christian Ziegler/Getty Images; bats roosting in a building sticker: Morley Read/123RF; ghost bat sticker: B. G. Thomson/Science Source.

BET YOU'VE GOT GOOD HEARING!

PARDON?